NorBy
the college mascot

A story by Nick Patton

For my favorite SNC co-worker (and mom) Cathy Patton

Published by St. Norbert College Press
St. Norbert College
100 Grant Street
De Pere, WI 54115

Library of Congress Control Number: 2013936022
ISBN 978-0-9851080-1-4

Summary: The St. Norbert mascot discovers what it is like to be a student, professor and president of the college.

Illustrations were created digitally in Adobe Photoshop.

Visit St. Norbert College online at **snc.edu**.
Visit the author at **nickpatton.com**.

NORBY the Green Knight was the mascot of St. NorBert college.

He spent his days spreading school spirit throughout the campus. Norby loved the college traditions.

He led the cheers at games ...

He guarded the school's magic victory bell. And he always had time for hugging babies and posing for pictures.

Norby loved being the mascot ...

... until one day right at the beginning of the school year, when the college held a big celebration. A student gave a speech to the new class. It was about learning how to change the world. Norby listened.

Norby thought, if he were given the opportunity, he would love to learn how to change the world. Leaning against the magic victory bell, he closed his eyes.

"I wish," Norby said to himself, **"I wish I was a student."**

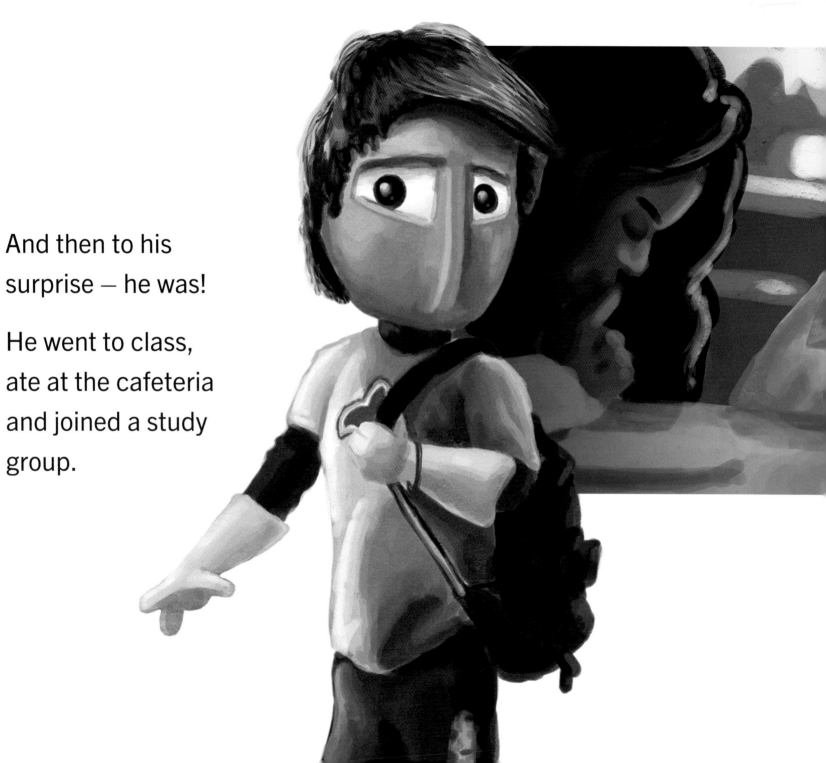

And then to his surprise — he was!

He went to class, ate at the cafeteria and joined a study group.

He even tried out for the rowing team.

Norby liked being a student ...

... until one day when his professor gave the class a pop quiz. Norby thought, if he were in charge, he wouldn't give pop quizzes.

"I Wish," Norby said to himself, **"I Wish I was a Professor."**

And then — he was!

Norby gave lectures on the lawn, enjoyed getting to know each of his students — and never gave a pop quiz.

Norby liked being a professor ...

... until one day when the college president came to see him. He told Norby that he shouldn't give his students smiley faces for grades.

Norby thought, if he were in charge, he'd allow smiley faces.

"I Wish," he said to himself, **"I Wish I Was the College President."**

And then — he was!

He went to important meetings,
signed diplomas and made
important decisions.

He held ice-cream parties every afternoon.

Norby liked being the college president ...

... until one day when a student came to see him. She told him that the college had no one to help carry on its traditions. Things just didn't seem the same, and the school had lost all its spirit.

Norby had quite enjoyed being a student, a professor and the college president. But he realized his college needed him to be something else ...

Norby leaned
up against the
magic victory bell
and thought.

"**I Wish,**" he said to himself,
"**I Wish I Was the College Mascot.**"

Then he opened
his eyes —
and he was!